A Home Under the Stars

Andy Chou Musser

little bigfoot
an imprint of sasquatch books
seattle, wa

Toby did not want to move to the city.

He missed his old home.

He missed climbing trees, taking quiet walks, and playing hide-and-seek in the garden.

Most of all, Toby missed seeing the stars
before bedtime.

He searched the night sky for the North Star.

But he couldn't see any stars in the city.

His parents tried to help. "Let's make our own stars."

"No!" shouted Toby.

"It's not the same."

Without the stars, Toby couldn't sleep.

From inside his closet, a voice growled,
"I can't sleep either."

"Oh!" Toby exclaimed. "A lion!"

"I need to find the North Star," the lion said.
"I'm lost without it to guide me home."

"Don't be sad," said Toby.

"I'll help you."

"The stars must be here somewhere," Toby said.

Together they searched for
the North Star.

"Do you hear that noise?"
asked the lion.

Someone was crying.

"What's wrong?" asked Toby.

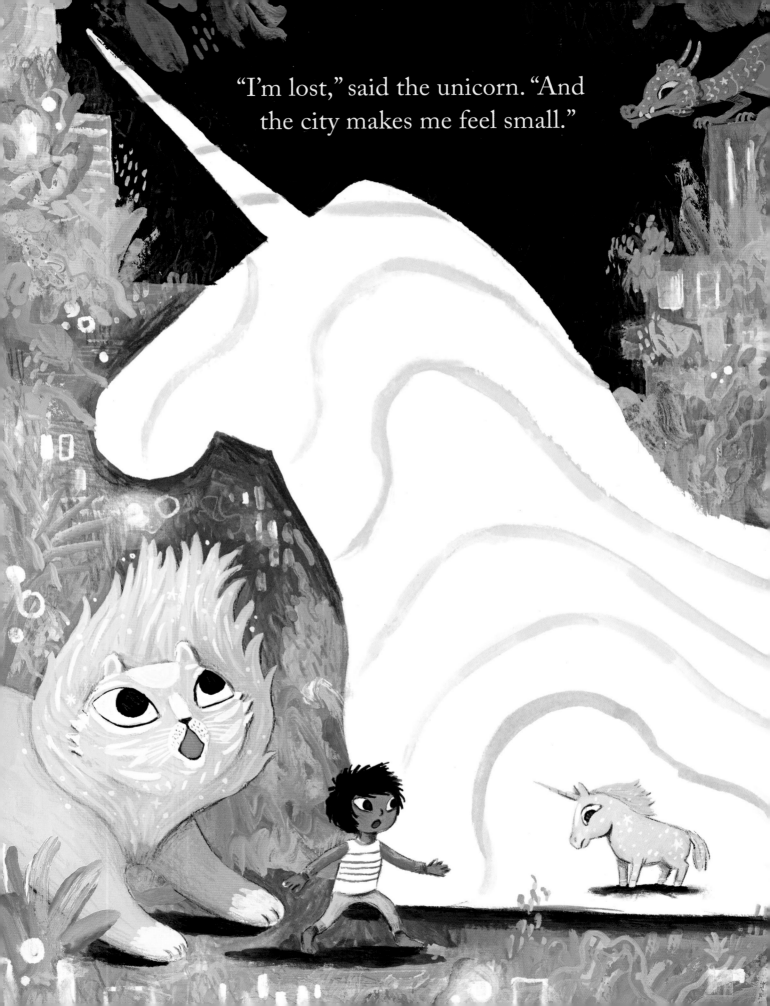

"I'm lost," said the unicorn. "And the city makes me feel small."

"Come with us," Toby said.

"We're looking for the North Star," the lion added. "It can show you the way home!"

As they searched the city, they found
more lost animals.

"I can't remember what home looks like
anymore," said the hare.

"I miss my friends," said the ram.

"The city is so noisy," said the eagle. "It scares me."

"Everything is different here," said the giraffe.
"Nothing feels right."

"Let's look for the North Star together," said Toby.
"It will guide you all home!"

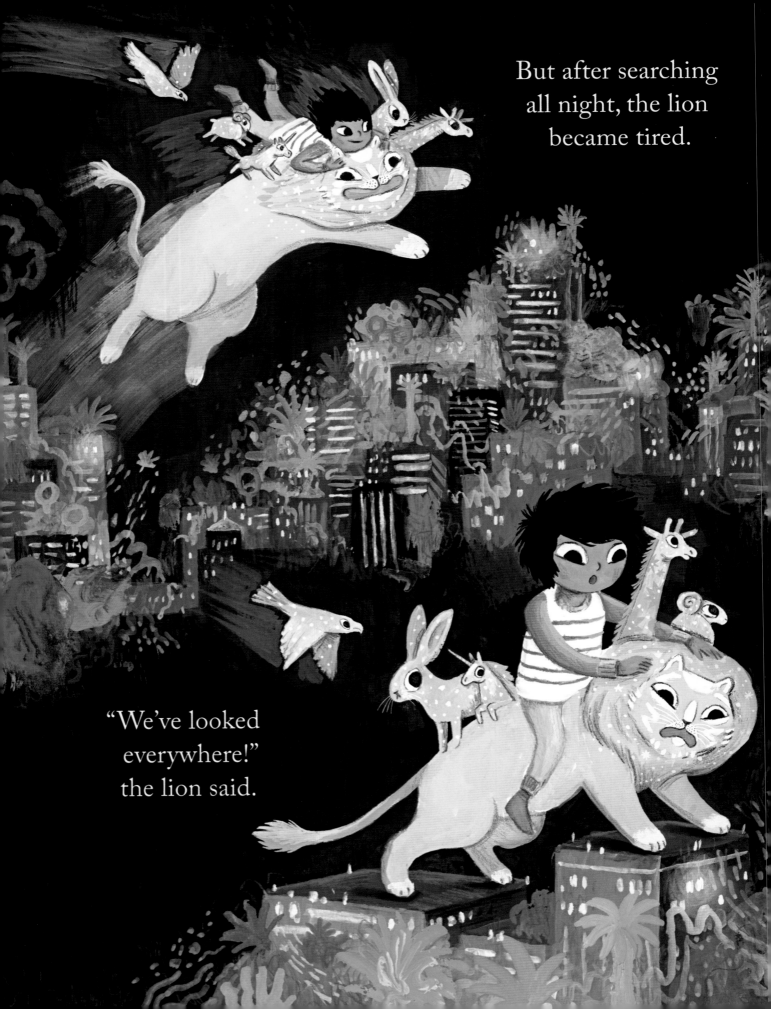

But after searching all night, the lion became tired.

"We've looked everywhere!" the lion said.

"What if we never find the North Star?"

"Please don't give up," said Toby. "I can't do this alone."

Suddenly, all the sounds of
the city stopped.

A deep rumble echoed down the streets.

"Hello?" Toby called. "Is someone there?"

A dragon lurched out of
the shadows and roared.
The city shook.

Toby froze. And then he saw something shimmer.

"Wait!" he shouted.

A broken star was blocking the
dragon's throat.

"Let me help you," Toby said.

"Thank you," the dragon bellowed.

As stars shot into the sky, everyone cheered. "You found the North Star!"

Toby joined them as they followed the star all the way home.

Monoceros

Lepus

Camelopardalis

Toby looked out at the stars, and his eyes grew heavy.
"If I go home, will I still be able to see you?" he asked.

"You may not be able to see us," said the lion,
"but we'll always be here for you."

That night, under the light of Toby's stars . . .

the city changed.

For Mom and Dad

Special thanks to Amy, Will, Ben, Hugh, Nina, Chris, Joy, Metal Pig,
and the numerous others who helped make this book possible.

Manufactured in China by Printplus Ltd.
in May 2021

LITTLE BIGFOOT with colophon is a registered
trademark of Penguin Random House LLC

25 24 23 22 21   9 8 7 6 5 4 3 2 1

Editors: Ben Clanton and Christy Cox
Production editor: Bridget Sweet
Designer: Anna Goldstein

ISBN: 978-1-63217-327-0

The art in this book was created using gouache paint and color pencils
on cold press watercolor paper, and assembled with digital magic.

Library of Congress Cataloging-in-Publication Data
Names: Musser, Andy Chou, author, illustrator.
Title: A home under the stars / Andy Chou Musser.
Description: Seattle : Little Bigfoot, [2021] | Audience: Ages 4-8. |
   Audience: Grades K-1. | Summary: When his family moves to the city, Toby
   misses seeing stars, but soon he meets some wild animals who all need
   the North Star to show their way home.
Identifiers: LCCN 2020054942 | ISBN 9781632173270 (hardcover)
Subjects: CYAC: Moving, Household--Fiction. | City and town life--Fiction.
   | Stars--Fiction. | Animals--Fiction. | Constellations--Fiction.
Classification: LCC PZ7.1.M8935 Hom 2021 | DDC [E]--dc23
LC record available at https://lccn.loc.gov/2020054942

Sasquatch Books
1904 Third Avenue, Suite 710
Seattle, WA 98101

SasquatchBooks.com